This book belongs to :

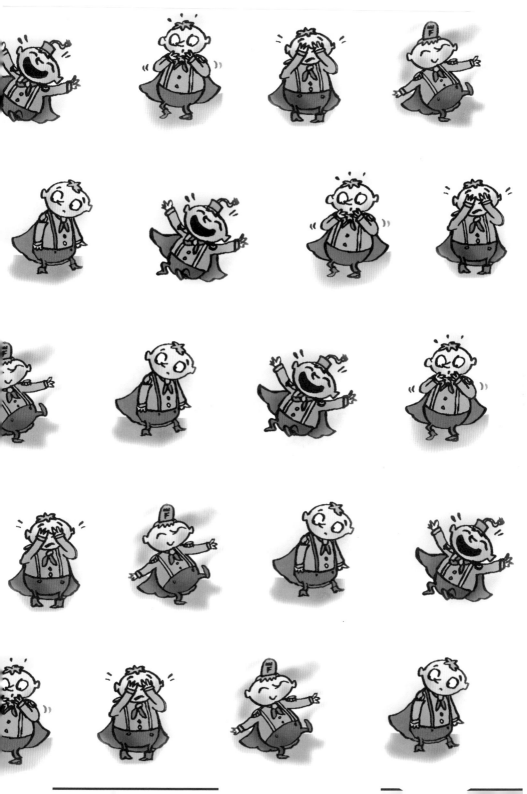

Zebedee Zing, Taster to the King

Zebedee Zing, Taster to the King

© 1998 Damon Burnard

ISBN 0713648856

First published in 1998

by A & C Black (Publishers) Ltd., England

國王的試吃官

Damon Burnard 著／繪

刊欣媒體營造工作室 譯

三民書局

Chapter One

Once upon a time, in a land three bus rides away, there lived a boy named Zebedee Zing.

Here's Zebedee, doing his most **favorite** thing in the whole, wide world...

第一章

　　從前，在很遠很遠，只有三路公車可以抵達的地方，住著一個叫做西庇太的男孩。

　　這就是西庇太，他正在做他最喜歡的事情……

once upon a time　從前（用於故事的開頭）

favorite [`fevrɪt]　[形]　最喜愛的

chomp [tʃɑmp]　[動]　（大聲地）咀嚼

guzzle [`gʌzl̩]　[動]　狂飲

chew [tʃu]　[動]　嚼

gulp [gʌlp]　[動]　大口吞食

Children want to be all kinds of things
when they grow up...

And Zebedee Zing?

每個小孩都希望長大後可以做自己想做的事情……

我要做一個小丑。

我要做廁所清潔人員。

我要當牙醫。

我要當獸醫。

我要成為一位狂人科學家……

……並且掌管世界！

那西庇太想做什麼呢？

clown [klaʊn] 名 小丑

dentist [ˋdɛntɪst] 名 牙醫

vet [vɛt] 名 獸醫 （＝veterinarian）

take over 接管

不論做什麼都好……

……只要可以大口大口地吃東西……

……咀嚼美味的食物……

……吃我想吃的東西……

……然後，一口氣吞下！

啊！

嗯！

Chapter Two

When Zebedee was old enough to leave school, he didn't go to Clown University, the Royal **Academy** of Toilet Cleaning, the College of Dentistry, the School for Vets or even the **Institute** of Mad Scientists in Zurich.

Zebedee became a waiter in a **posh** restaurant **instead**!

第二章

西庇太從學校畢業後，並沒有去上小丑大學、皇家廁所清潔學院、牙醫學院或獸醫學校，也沒有到蘇黎士的狂人科學機構做研究。

西庇太到一家豪華的餐廳當服務生！

啊！今日的蟲蟲特餐！

academy [əˋkædəmɪ] 名 學院

institute [ˋɪnstə,tjut] 名 機構

posh [pɑʃ] 形 豪華的

instead [ɪnˋstɛd] 副 取而代之地

This restaurant was so posh, even the rats in the kitchen spoke **French**!

Zebedee loved being a waiter. The trouble was the food smelt so good, he could never **resist** taking a **nibble**...

這家餐廳非常豪華，連廚房裏的老鼠都是說法文的。

唉呀！一個魚頭！

真幸運！

太棒了！

西庇太很喜歡服務生這個工作。可是問題是食物聞起來太好吃了，常常會讓他忍不住偷嘗一口……

嗯！好吃！

French [frɛntʃ] 名 法語

resist [rɪˋzɪst] 動 忍得住（誘惑等）

nibble [ˋnɪbl̩] 名 咬一口

tasty [ˋtestɪ] 形 好吃的

But the little nibble would **turn into** a BIG **BITE**...

...and by the time he **reached** the hungry **diner**, there'd be nothing left at all!

Zebedee didn't work at the posh restaurant for very long!

不過，一小口慢慢地變成一大口……

……然後當他把食物送到饑餓的客人桌上時，盤子裏已經一點兒食物也不剩了！

你的晚餐，先生。嗝！

嗯！在哪裡呢？

因此，西庇太並沒有在這家豪華的餐廳工作多久。

再見！

turn into 變成

bite [baɪt] 名 咬一口

reach [ritʃ] 動 到達

diner [ˋdaɪnɚ] 名 用餐者

belch [bɛltʃ] 動 打嗝

Next, Zebedee got a job **delivering** pizzas...

But the pizzas smelt so good, he could never resist taking a little bite...

The little bite would turn into lots of BIG BITES...

接著，西庇太找到一個外送披薩的工作……

芝士的味道

可是披薩聞起來也很好吃，他還是會忍不住偷嘗一

塊……

啊，這是義式火腿的披薩！

我只要吃一小口就好了！

一小口又慢慢地變成了一大口……

deliver [dɪˋlɪvɚ] 動 遞送

pepperoni [͵pɛpəˋronɪ] 名

　義大利風味的辛辣硬香腸

...and by the time he reached his **destination**, there'd be nothing left at all!

Zebedee didn't deliver pizzas for very long!

……在他到達目的地之前，披薩就已經吃得一點兒也不剩了。

　　嗝！先生，你的披薩！

　　啊！只剩披薩屑了！

　　當然，送披薩的工作也做不了太久。

destination [ˌdɛstəˋneʃən] 名 目的地

burp [bɝp] 動 打嗝

crumb [krʌm] 名 （麵包、蛋糕等的）碎屑

Next Zebedee got a job at the **Museum** of Natural History.

But looking at **dinosaur** bones all day made him very hungry. One afternoon, Zebedee couldn't resist taking one **teeny-weeny**, **teensy-weensy** bone to **gnaw** on...

接著，西庇太到自然歷史博物館工作。

整天望著恐龍的骨頭讓西庇太覺得餓極了。有一天下午，他實在忍不住了，於是拿起一塊小小、小小的骨頭咬了起來……

我想一定不會有人發現到這一小塊不見了！

museum [mju`ziəm] 名 博物館

dinosaur [`daɪnə,sɔr] 名 恐龍

teeny-weeny [`tɪnɪ`winɪ],

teensy-weensy [`tinzɪ`winzɪ] 形 極小的（=tiny）

gnaw [nɔ] 動 啃咬；嚼《on》

miss [mɪs] 動 發現…不見了

itsy-bitsy [`ɪtsɪ`bɪtsɪ] 形 小小的

Unfortunately, it turned out to be a very important, teeny-weeny, teensy-weensy bone indeed!

Zebedee didn't work at the Museum of Natural History for very long!

不幸的是，那一小塊正是非常重要，無它不可的骨頭！

　　西庇太當然也沒能在博物館工作多久！

unfortunately [ʌn`fɔrtʃənətlɪ] 副 不幸地

Chapter Three

Before long, there was only one job left for Zebedee to do. He had to wear a bright orange **suit** and a little orange, **triangular** hat, and he had to stand very, very **still**...

Zebedee was a traffic cone on the motorway!

Sadly for Zebedee, there was nothing on the motorway to chomp, or chew, or guzzle — **except for** the **occasional** bug!

第三章

　　很快地，西庇太只剩下一個工作可以做了。他得穿上鮮橘色的衣服、戴上一頂橘色的三角小帽，然後要靜靜地站著……

　　西庇太的工作是扮成高速公路上的交通三角錐！

　　可憐的西庇太，在高速公路上可沒什麼東西可以吃——除了偶爾飛來的小蟲子。

suit [sut] 名 套裝

triangular [traɪˋæŋgjələ˞] 形 三角形的

still [stɪl] 副 靜止不動地

except for... 除了…之外

occasional [əˋkeʒənl] 形 偶爾的

What's more, Zebedee only earned enough money to buy second-hand eggs and old chickens' livers for his supper!

Zebedee Zing was a **miserable** thing!

His one **delight** was to visit the Royal **Palace**, which stood **regal** and **palatial** on the other side of town.

而且，更可憐的是，西庇太賺的錢只夠買二手雞蛋和老雞肝來當晚餐！

這真是垃圾！

悲慘的西庇太！

唯一能夠讓他感到高興的，就是去參觀皇宮——這座華麗的皇宮就蓋在小鎮的另一邊。

miserable [`mɪzrəbl̩] 形 可憐的

delight [dɪ`laɪt] 名 使人高興的事；高興

palace [`pælɪs] 名 宮殿

regal [`rigl̩] 形 堂皇的

palatial [pə`leʃəl] 形 宮殿似的

Zebedee would **tippy-toe** over to the kitchen window and watch while a dozen cooks prepared **dazzlingly** delightful delicious **delicacies**...

'**Trembling** truffles!' **exclaimed** Zebedee.

Whoever lives here must be the Happiest Person Ever!

西庇太會踮著腳、悄悄走到廚房的窗邊，看著廚房裏的十二位廚師準備豐富美味的食物……

「松露吧！」西庇太興奮地叫了起來。

不論住在這兒的是誰，他一定是有史以來最快樂的人！

tippy-toe [`tɪpɪˌto] 動 躡手躡腳地走

（=tiptoe）

dazzlingly [`dæzl̩ɪŋlɪ] 副 令人目眩地

delicacy [`dɛləkəsɪ] 名 佳肴，美食

trembling [`trɛmblɪŋ] 形 顫抖的

exclaim [ɪk`sklem] 動 驚叫

Chapter Four

In that palace, lived a king. This is the Royal **Portrait** of him.

In fact, he looked more like this...

Like most kings, the king had big ears. This was a good thing, as without them, his **crown** would **slide** down, and he'd **end up** looking like this...

第四章

　　皇宮裏住著一位國王，這是國王的肖像。

　　實際上，國王本人應該是這個樣子⋯⋯

　　跟大部分的國王一樣，這位國王也有一對大耳朵。這是一件好事，因為如果沒有大耳朵，皇冠就會滑下來，然後會變成這樣⋯⋯

　　救命啊！

　　我看不見了！

portrait [`portret] 名 肖像

crown [kraun] 名 皇冠

slide [slaɪd] 動 滑動

end up　最後變成

The king had a whole
room, just for his toys...

He had his own,
private cinema...

He swam in a pool
of chocolate milk...

...and he had
those twelve cooks
I **mentioned** on
page 26...

國王有一個裝滿玩具的房間……

跟一間私人的電影院……

他還可以在巧克力牛奶的游泳池中游泳……

……國王還擁有十二名廚師，就是我在２６頁提到的那十二位……

private [`praɪvɪt] 形 私有的

cinema [`sɪnəmə] 名 電影院

mention [`mɛnʃən] 動 提到

And yet, **despite** all this, the king was not the Happiest Person Ever. Instead, he was the Most **Suspicious**.

For a start, he didn't believe people when they were nice to him.

He **imagined** they said **nasty** things about him behind his back, and **hatched** evil **plots** against him.

雖然這樣，國王卻不是「有史以來最快樂的人」，反而是個「最多疑的人」。

　　從一開始，他就不相信別人對他的好意。

　　我是方糖啊！

　　嗨，國王！

　　有什麼事嗎？

　　哼！

　　國王好！

　　他認為別人都在他的背後說他的壞話、設計他。

despite [dɪˋspaɪt] 介 儘管

suspicious [səˋspɪʃəs] 形 多疑的

imagine [ɪˋmædʒɪn] 動 想像

nasty [ˋnæstɪ] 形 不道德的

hatch [hætʃ] 動 策劃

plot [plɑt] 名 陰謀

'Humph!' he'd think. 'They're **jealous** of my palace and my toys and my pool and my cinema and my cooks.'

The king was especially worried about someone stealing his crown while he slept. And so he **spread** a **rumor** that a **ferocious** man-eating lion **guarded** him at night.

However, like most rumors, this rumor was not 100% true...

「哼！」他想，「他們一定是忌妒我的皇宮、我的玩具、游泳池、電影院、還有廚師。」

他們最忌妒的是……

……我的皇冠！

因為國王很擔心有人會在他睡覺時偷走皇冠。所以，他散播謠言說：晚上有一隻兇猛，而且會吃人的獅子保護著他。

當然，就像大多數的謠言一樣，這個謠言也不是百分之百真實……

jealous [`dʒɛləs] 形 妒忌的
spread [sprɛd] 動 散播
rumor [`rumɚ] 名 謠傳
ferocious [fə`roʃəs] 形 兇暴的
guard [gɑrd] 動 守衛

The only lion the king really had was the soft and **fuzzy** one that sat upon his **pillow**.

The king called it Lion, except when he was sure that no-one was listening, and then he called it Liony-Wiony. He'd hold Liony-Wiony **tight** through the dark, inky night, when the **shadows** came a-**creeping**. It made him feel less afraid.

國王唯一真正擁有的一隻獅子，是一隻放在枕邊的絨毛玩具。

平常國王稱呼它「獅子」，只有在確定四下無人時才叫它「獅寶寶」。在黑夜悄悄來臨的時候，他只有緊緊地抱著獅寶寶，渡過黑漆漆的夜晚，這樣他的恐懼才能減少一些。

fuzzy [`fʌzɪ] 形 毛茸茸的

pillow [`pɪlo] 名 枕頭

tight [taɪt] 副 緊緊地

shadow [`ʃædo] 名 暮色；昏暗

creep [krip] 動 悄悄靠近

註："a-"，後接動名詞，表示「動作正在進行」。

Chapter Five

Just lately, the king had grown especially suspicious of his cooks. 'What if they **slip** some sleeping potion into my food?' he thought.

To be on the safe side, the king ate very little of the **sumptuous treats** that the cooks prepared...

He was indeed a **skinny** kind of king.

第五章

　　最近，國王對廚師起了疑心。他想，「他們會不會在我的食物裏摻了安眠藥？」

　　那他們就會偷走我的皇冠！

　　為了安全起見，國王對廚師們準備的豐富食物，都只吃一點點……

　　他變成一位很瘦很瘦的國王。

slip [slɪp] 動 偷偷塞進 《into》

sumptuous [`sʌmptʃʊəs] 形 奢華的

treat [trit] 名 款待

skinny [`skɪnɪ] 形 皮包骨的

As an extra **precaution**, the king would tippy-toe out of the back door and **spy** on the cooks through the kitchen window.

But one day, to his surprise...

...someone was there ahead of him!

除此之外，國王還會悄悄地來到後門邊，從廚房的窗戶監視著廚師。

　　可是，有一天，出乎他的意料……

　　……居然已經有人先他一步來到窗邊了！

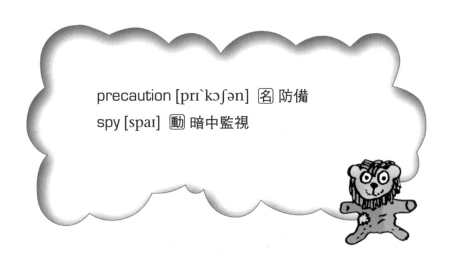

precaution [prɪˋkɔʃən] 名 防備

spy [spaɪ] 動 暗中監視

Chapter Six

'YOU THERE!' said the king, in the **bravest** voice he could **muster**.

'No,' said Zebedee. 'I'm not!'

第六章

「你在這裏做什麼？」國王用聽起來最勇敢的聲音問。

你是不是想設計我？

「不是，」西庇太說。「我沒有！」

那麼，你有陰謀？

沒有？

存心不良？

不是。

真的嗎？

當然。

brave [brev] 形 勇敢的

muster [`mʌstɚ] 動 鼓起

plot [plɑt] 動 策劃陰謀

scheme [skim] 動 策劃陰謀

positive [`pɑzətɪv] 形 確定的

'Because if you *are* plotting against me, I'll have to set my lion on you,' said the king.

But Zebedee wasn't listening. He was too busy **staring** into the kitchen, his eyes as wide as **saucers**.

'Galloping **gorgonzola!**' he **gushed**.

「如果你敢設計我，我就叫我的獅子攻擊你。」國王說。

知道了嗎？

不過西庇太沒有在聽國王說話，他正忙著注意廚房裏的動靜，兩隻眼睛瞪得像托盤一樣大。

「乳酪！」他熱情地叫著。

好想嘗一口那些食物喔！

stare [stɛr] 動 目不轉睛地看

saucer [`sɔsɚ] 名 茶碟

gorgonzola [,gɔrgən`zolə] 名
一種產於義大利的乳酪

gush [gʌʃ] 動 誇張地說

Suddenly the king had an idea.

'What would I have to do, exactly?' asked Zebedee.

The king explained that his job would be to taste the king's food before he did, to make sure it was safe to eat.

你真的想嗎？

當然想！

國王忽然想到了一個好主意。

喂！你想不想當國王的試吃官啊？

想不想？我非常願意呢！

「可是我到底該做些什麼事呢？」西庇太問。

國王向西庇太說明：這個工作就是先試吃國王要吃的食物，確定食物是安全的。

'That way,' added the king, 'I wouldn't have to spy on the cooks any more...'

'I'll do it!' **yelled** Zebedee, **leaping joyously** into the air.

But the job wasn't his. Not yet.

「這樣一來，」國王接著說，「我就不用再監視廚師了⋯⋯」

那我就會有更多的時間來懷疑別的事了。

「我願意做這份工作！」西庇太叫著，一邊高興地跳了起來。

哎！小心我的排水口！

西庇太還沒正式獲得這份工作呢！

free [fri] 動 釋放

yell [jɛl] 動 大叫

leap [lip] 動 跳

joyously [`dʒɔɪəslɪ] 副 高興地

Not only was the king:

a) skinny, and

b) suspicious, he was also

c) **cautious**, and

d) **officious**.

And so, before making Zebedee his **Official** Taster, the king gave him a Royal Taster's Test.

Zebedee never thought that a test could be so much fun!

國王不但

　a. 很瘦很瘦，還

　b. 很多疑，而且

　c. 非常小心，又

　d. 愛管閒事。

　所以，在任命西庇太為正式的試吃官前，國王先對西庇太進行「皇家試吃官考試」。

　西庇太從來沒想到考試會這麼有趣！

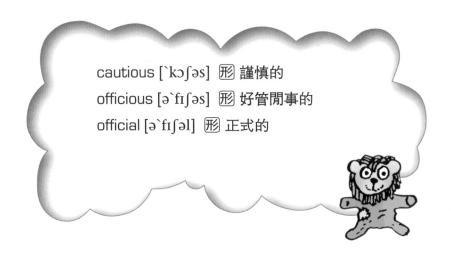

cautious [`kɔʃəs] 形 謹慎的

officious [ə`fɪʃəs] 形 好管閒事的

official [ə`fɪʃəl] 形 正式的

Here's Zebedee's report card; as you can see, he did well on everything...well, nearly everything!

Effort 10
Enthusiasm 10
Zeal 10
Ardor 10
Vigor 10
Fervor..................10
Thoroughness...10
Speed..................10
Energy..................10
Table Manners.....0
                    90
TOTAL............... 100

And so, in a single day, Zebedee went from being a chicken-liver chomping, second-hand egg eating, bug-crunching traffic cone, to Zebedee Zing, Taster to the King!

這就是西庇太的成績單,看得出來他每一項……幾乎是每一項啦……都表現得很好。

　　所以,不過一天,西庇太從一個在高速公路上扮交通三角錐,偶爾吃吃小蟲子,只能以雞肝和二手雞蛋當食物的人,變成了國王的試吃官!

effort [ˋɛfɚt] 名 努力

enthusiasm [ɪnˋθjuzɪˌæzəm] 名 熱情

zeal [zil] 名 熱忱

ardor [ˋɑrdɚ] 名 熱心

vigor [ˋvɪgɚ] 名 活力

fervor [ˋfɝvɚ] 名 熱誠

Chapter Seven

Here's Zebedee in his Royal Taster's **Uniform**...

Zebedee loved his new job. Being a traffic cone had been very lonely—especially in the rain and the cold. But now he could spend the day **strolling** through the king's lovely, warm palace.

第七章

這是西庇太穿著皇家試吃官制服的樣子……

帽子上的'T'是「試吃官」的意思……

……而上面的皇冠代表我是國王的試吃官！

西庇太很喜歡他的新工作。扮交通三角錐是很寂寞的——尤其是下雨或天冷的時候。可是現在他卻可以整天在可愛又溫暖的皇宮裏閒逛。

uniform [`junə͵fɔrm] 名 制服

stand for 表示

stroll [strol] 動 閒逛

He also liked spending time with the king, even if he was **moody** and **grouchy**, and didn't know how to share...

But most of all, Zebedee loved tasting the cooks' **fabulous** food; their chips, **for example**, were **perfect!**

他也很喜歡和國王在一起，即使國王心情沮喪不高興，不知道怎麼和別人分享……

嗨，國王！我可以玩嗎？

不行！

而西庇太最——最——喜歡的就是試吃廚師做的食物了，比如，炸薯條就很棒！

不太厚，也不會太薄

炸成可愛的金黃色

很脆，又不會太脆

moody [`mudɪ] 形 憂鬱的

grouchy [`graʊtʃɪ] 形 愛抱怨的

fabulous [`fæbjələs] 形 極佳的；驚人的

for example 比如說

perfect [`pɝfɪkt] 形 完美無缺的

At first the king was very **pleased** with himself, for in Zebedee he had found the World's Greatest Taster.

The trouble was, Zebedee was so Great, there was never much left for the king to taste!

剛開始，國王對西庇太很滿意，覺得他是全世界最好的試吃官。

　　沾沾自喜的國王

　　問題是，西庇太實在太厲害了，幾乎從來都沒什麼食物可以留給國王吃！

　　吃吧，國王！食物沒問題！

pleased [plizd] 形 高興的

self-satisfaction [ˌsɛlfsætɪsˋfækʃən]

　　名 沾沾自喜

go ahead 繼續

The king became so very skinny, when he stood **sideways**, he was nearly **invisible**.

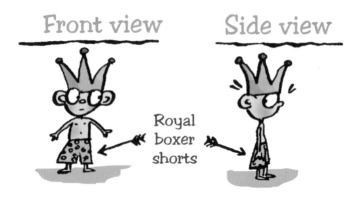

Front view   Side view

Royal boxer shorts

Each night he went to bed a little hungrier, and his **tummy growled** a little louder than the night before.

'Oh well!' **grumbled** the king.

It's a small price to pay, to know that my crown is safe!

Grrr!

But deep down, he wasn't so sure...

國王越來越瘦了，從側面看過去，幾乎看不見國王。

每天晚上，國王帶著越來越餓的肚子上床睡覺，他的肚子咕嚕咕嚕地，一天叫得比一天大聲。

「哎喔！」國王抱怨著。

為了皇冠的安全，這點小小的代價不算什麼。

可是，慢慢地，他不那麼認為了……

sideways [ˋsaɪdˏwez] 副 側向一邊地

invisible [ɪnˋvɪzəbḷ] 形 看不見的

tummy [ˋtʌmɪ] 名 肚子

growl [graʊl] 動 咆哮

grumble [ˋgrʌmbḷ] 動 抱怨

Chapter Eight

As the days went by, the king got hungrier and hungrier. By the time his birthday **came around**, he was too hungry to remember which one it was. He'd just **narrowed** it **down** to either his ninth, or his forty-second, when the Head Chef **burst** in.

'**In honor of** this glorious **occasion**,' the Head Chef cheerfully **announced**, 'we have prepared a birthday surprise!' And with that, he clicked his fingers. Twice.

第八章

　　日子一天一天過去，國王也越來越餓。在國王生日的前幾天，他已經餓得記不清自己的生日是哪一天。當主廚衝進來時，國王正弄不清楚這到底是他第九個生日或是第四十二個。

　　生日快樂，國王！

　　喔，謝謝！

　　「為了慶祝這個特別的日子，」主廚高興地宣布，「我們為您準備了一個生日驚喜！」然後，他彈了二下手指。

come around　（從遠方）來到；到達

narrow [`næro] 動 使變窄

narrow down　縮減

burst [bɝst] 動 突然出現

in honor of... 為了祝賀…

occasion [ə`keʒən] 名 值得祝賀的時候

announce [ə`nauns] 動 宣布

In came the cooks, carrying a huge gift-wrapped THING.

'Uh-oh chungo!' thought the king. 'What can it be?'

廚師們帶著一個包裝好的——大——禮物進來。

「哇一哇！」國王想。「那會是什麼呢？」

With trembling fingers he **undid** the bow,
to **reveal**...

可能是一顆炸彈……

或者是二顆炸彈！

他用發抖的手指解開蝴蝶結……

一個蛋糕！

我想他喜歡這個禮物。

undo [ʌn`du] 動 解開

　（過去式 undid [ʌn`dɪd]；

　過去分詞 undone [ʌn`dʌn]）

reveal [rɪ`vil] 動 揭示

'That's right, Your Royal Skinnyness!' said the Head Chef. 'A cake! And on top we've written "We love you" in chocolate chips!'

「沒錯，皮包骨的國王陛下！」主廚說。「是一個蛋糕！而且我們在最上面用巧克力片寫著『我們愛你』。」

是嗎？

是的！而且城裡的每一個人都用粉紅色的糖霜簽了名。

他們真的這麼做了？

真的！

哎呀！

The king's heart **melted** like a **scoop** of ice cream on a dragon's tongue.

'Oh thank you!' he cried.

Not only did the king forget about being suspicious, he couldn't even remember why he had been **in the first place**! He was so pleased he gave everyone the day off, then away he ran to **fetch** a spoon. Oh, and a ladder.

國王的心慢慢融化，就像一球冰淇淋在噴火龍的舌頭上融化一樣。

「謝謝！」他大叫。

這真是有史以來最好的生日蛋糕！

不用客氣！

國王不但忘記懷疑，他甚至不記得自己是怎麼開始起疑心病的！他高興地讓每個人放一天假，然後跑去拿一支湯匙回來，喔，還有一把梯子。

melt [mɛlt] 動 融化
scoop [skup] 名 舀一次的量
in the first place 本來
fetch [fɛtʃ] 動 帶來

Just as the king **was about to dive** into the cake, in rushed Zebedee.

'WAIT!' he **screamed**.

SHOULDN'T I TASTE IT FIRST?

For once, the king wasn't sure.

就在國王準備跳進蛋糕裏時，西庇太衝了進來。

「等一下！」他大叫。

不用我先試吃嗎？

這一次，國王猶豫了一下。

be about to（do）正想要做…

dive [daɪv] 動 跳進《into》

scream [skrim] 動 尖叫

for once 僅此一次

'No, I don't think so,' he said.

「不，我想不用。」他說。

還是謝謝你！

可是如果廚師放了什麼噁心的東西呢？

或是發笑劑呢？

喔！他們不會做那種事的。

你確定嗎？

呃……是……

我確定……

'What, **absolutely** sure?' asked Zebedee.

'Maybe Zebedee is right!' thought the king. '**After all**, something bad **is bound to** happen to me on my birthday!'

He climbed down the ladder and **weighed up the pros and cons, the fors and againsts** and the pluses and minuses.

「什麼？完全確定嗎？」西庇太反問。

百分之百確定？

嗯，可能只有百分之九十九點九！

「或許西庇太是對的！」國王這麼想。「畢竟，在我生日這一天還是可能會有不好的事發生。」

他爬下梯子，來來回回、反反覆覆地仔細想了想。

absolutely [ˋæbsə͵lutlɪ] 副 完全地

after all 畢竟；到底

be bound to（do）必定會…

weigh [we] 動 秤重

weigh up 慎重考慮

the pros and cons 利害得失

the fors and againsts 贊成與反對

At last he decided that Zebedee should taste it.

'I **promise**!' promised Zebedee. 'Now, please get out of my way!' he cried, and he **jumped** into the cake, head first.

最後，他決定讓西庇太先試吃。

可是不能吃太多喲！

呀呼！

「我保證！」西庇太答應著。「現在，請別擋著我的路。」他叫著，然後一頭跳進蛋糕裏。

promise [ˋprɑmɪs] 動 保證

jump [dʒʌmp] 動 跳起

Chapter Nine

'Well?' asked the king, after a while.

'I need a few more **mouthfuls**!' said Zebedee.

A little later, the king asked him again.

第九章

「怎麼樣？」過了一會兒，國王問。

蛋糕安全嗎？我可以吃了嗎？

嗯！我還不確定！

「我還得再吃幾口。」西庇太說。

過了一會兒，國王又再問一次。

可以了嗎？

嗯—嗯！我還是不能確定。

mouthful [`mauθ,ful] 名 一口的量

And so it went on, and on, until there was just one crumb left.

'Oh no!' thought the king.

'MY CAKE!'

He made a **dash** for the crumb...

desperate leap!

But Zebedee got there first!

所以，西庇太繼續吃、國王繼續問，直到只剩下一個蛋糕屑。

「喔，不！」國王心想。

「我的蛋糕！」

他趕緊衝了過去……

可是西庇太比他早了一步。

dash [dæʃ] 名 衝

desperate [ˋdɛsprɪt] 形 不顧一切的

In **desperation** the king watched as
Zebedee **flicked** the crumb into his mouth.

'DELICIOUS!' he exclaimed. And then he
noticed the king, lying on the empty plate.

'Oh, hello!' he said.

國王絕望地看著西庇太把最後一塊蛋糕屑彈進嘴裏
……

「好吃！」他大聲說。然後，他注意到國王正躺在
空空的蛋糕盤裏。

「喔，哈囉！」他說。

你今天還快樂嗎？

desperation [ˌdɛspəˋreʃn] 名 絕望

flick [flɪk] 動 輕彈

Chapter Ten

Normally the king was a quiet kind of king, and even when he was **cross** he'd just **smoulder** and **fume** like a damp rag over a dull flame.

But at that moment he was Extra-specially Super Cross!

第十章

　　國王平常是一個很安靜的人，即使發怒也不會表現出來，就像放在餘火上的溼抹布一樣，自己生著悶氣。

　　但此時他卻變得非常——非常——生氣。

　　貪心的人！

　　好吃鬼！

cross [krɔs] 形 生氣的

smoulder [`smoldɚ] 動 壓抑

fume [fjum] 動 發怒

greedy [`gridɪ] 形 貪得無厭的

He went all red in the face and **bounced** about, **up and down** and all around, shouting all the while...

Zebedee felt terrible. He was filled with **remorse** (see **diagram**).

Diagram: Zebedee filled with remorse

level of remorse

NB: shaded area represents remorse.

他氣得滿臉通紅，不停地跳來跳去，一邊大叫著……

西庇太感到很難過。他感到自責（如圖）。

圖：西庇太非常自責

自責的程度

註：陰影部分代表自責。

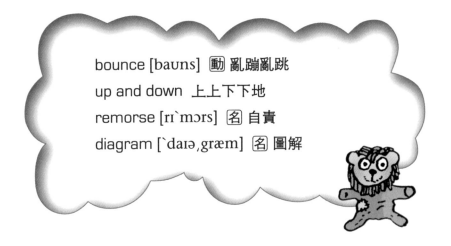

bounce [baʊns] 勔 亂蹦亂跳

up and down 上上下下地

remorse [rɪˋmɔrs] 名 自責

diagram [ˋdaɪəˏgræm] 名 圖解

'I'm sorry, King!' he cried.

And with that he **snatched** the hat from Zebedee's head—the hat Zebedee loved so much—and jumped on it.

「國王，對不起！」他叫著。

你說說話嘛！

說說話？你自己應該知道！

如果你不說，我怎麼會知道？

如果我不說，你就不知道，那你就自己猜！

接著，國王搶走西庇太的帽子——那頂他最喜愛的帽子——還在帽子上用力跳著。

snatch [snætʃ] 動 搶奪

Jumping on it once would've been bad enough, but the king jumped on it over and over again, until Zebedee couldn't **bear** to watch.

'GET OUT!' shouted the king.

Zebedee Zing **made for** the door, for he was Taster to the King no more!

跳一次還不夠，國王不斷地在帽子上又踩又跳的，直到西庇太不忍心看下去。

　　「出去！」國王大叫著。

　　你被開除了！

　　西庇太朝門口走去，因為他再也不是國王的試吃官了！

bear [bɛr] 動 忍受

make for... 朝…方向前進

Chapter Eleven

'**Typical!**' grumbled the king.

He was so hungry and cross, he decided that there was nothing left to do but wait until bed-time.

Now his palace was empty, it was an **awfully** long and quiet wait — especially without Zebedee bounding and **crashing** about!

第十一章

「常有的事！」國王抱怨。

今天是我的生日……

……可是我連一口蛋糕都沒吃到！

他又餓又生氣，想想也沒別的事情可以做，只好等著睡覺。

唉！

這個時候，皇宮裏空無一人，這是一個非常漫長又很安靜的等待──尤其是少了西庇太在一旁橫衝直撞地跑來跑去。

typical [ˋtɪpɪkl̩] 形 典型的
awfully [ˋɔflɪ] 副 非常
crash [kræʃ] 動 衝撞

At last the clock struck bed-time, and the king **crabbily** climbed the stairs. 'I **bet** someone tries to steal my crown tonight!' he thought.

And you know what? He was right!

That dark and inky night, just as he was **dropping off** to sleep, a **burglar** stole through his window...

最後，上床的鐘聲終於響了，國王憤怒地爬上樓梯。「我猜，今天晚上一定會有人來偷我的皇冠！」他想。

早就不足為奇了！

然後，你猜發生什麼事？──國王說對了！

黑漆漆的夜晚，就在國王睡著以後，一個小偷悄悄地從窗戶爬了進來……

嘿嘿！

crabbily [ˋkræbɪlɪ] 副 脾氣暴躁地

bet [bɛt] 動 打賭

drop off 不知不覺地睡著

burglar [ˋbɝglɚ] 名 夜賊

'Hello, King!' said the burglar.

'Oh, h-hello!' said the king.

'Oh,' said the king.

'No,' said the burglar, again.

「哈囉，國王！」小偷對國王說。

「喔―，哈―囉！」國王回答。

你是來祝我生日快樂的嗎？

不！

「喔──！」國王說。

嗯―，那麼你是來替我把枕頭拍鬆的嗎？

「不是！」小偷又說。

fluff [flʌf] 動 使蓬鬆 《up》

'Oh,' said the king. 'I thought as much!'

And then the burglar saw Liony-Wiony.

'Ha ha!' he **sniggered**.

'I've a real lion too!' said the king, trying
not to sound **nervous**, which was difficult,
because he was very nervous indeed.

'And he'll p-**pounce** at any moment!'

我是來偷你的皇冠的！

「喔！我想也是。」國王說。

接著小偷看見了「獅寶寶」。

「哈哈！」他偷笑著。

這就是我聽說的、會吃人的護王獅囉！

嗯一，其實——不是。

「我還有一隻真的獅子！」國王試著用聽起來不緊張的聲音回答，但是那並不容易，因為他真的非常緊張。

「牠隨時可能會撲過來！」

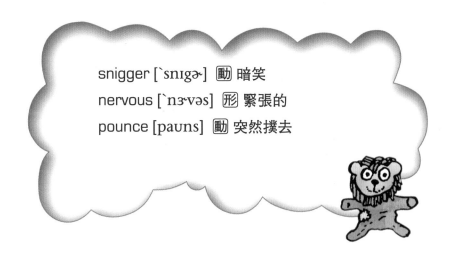

snigger [`snɪgɚ] 動 暗笑

nervous [`nɝvəs] 形 緊張的

pounce [paʊns] 動 突然撲去

The burglar **roared** with laughter. He snatched up Liony-Wiony and **pranced** around the room, chanting in a singy-songy voice.

'Ha! Ha! Ha!' he **mocked**, when he'd finished. 'What a silly king you are!' But as he reached out to grab the king's crown...

...there was a loud...

小偷又笑又吼。他抓起獅寶寶，在房間裏大步走來走去，還一邊用唱歌的音調哼著。

國王抱著獅子睡覺！

一隻柔軟的絨毛玩具！

「哈！哈！哈！」他唱完歌後，還大聲嘲笑國王。「多愚蠢的國王啊！」但是當他準備奪走國王的皇冠時……

……出現一聲大聲的……

roar [ror] 動 （野獸等）吼叫

prance [præns] 動 大搖大擺地行走

mock [mɑk] 動 嘲笑

'Eeek!' **squealed** the burglar.

Then...

The burglar turned as white as a sheet and **trembled** like a plate of jelly rollerblading down a cobblestone street.

「噫！」小偷尖叫著。

那是什麼聲音？

然後⋯⋯

又一聲吼叫！

那個小偷嚇壞了，臉色蒼白得像一張紙，而且全身抖得像一盤在石子路上溜冰的果凍一樣。

squeal [skwil] 動 發出長而尖的叫聲

tremble [`trɛmbḷ] 動 顫抖

'I'm **getting out of** here!' screamed the burglar. He turned on his heels and leapt out of the window.

是獅子！

「我要離開這裏！」小偷尖叫著，轉身就跳出窗戶。

get out of... 從…出來；擺脫…

Chapter Twelve

SO...

Did the king have a fierce, man-eating lion after all?

NO!

It was the **rowdy rumblings** of a royal tummy that the robber **mistook** for a **ravenous** roar! Really!

How felicitous!

said the king, which is a fancy way of saying that the whole thing was very lucky indeed.

第十二章

國王真的擁有一隻兇猛的、會吃人的獅子嗎？

不！

那只是饑餓的國王的肚子所發出來的聲音。小偷誤以為是獅子的吼叫聲！真的！

多麼巧啊！

國王俏皮地說著，這件事確實很幸運。

rowdy [`raʊdɪ] 形 粗暴的

rumbling [`rʌmblɪŋ] 名 轆轆聲

mistake [mə`stek] 動 誤認 《for》

ravenous [`rævənəs] 形 非常饑餓的

felicitous [fə`lɪsətəs] 形 巧妙的

'Thank goodness for Zebedee Zing!' he thought.

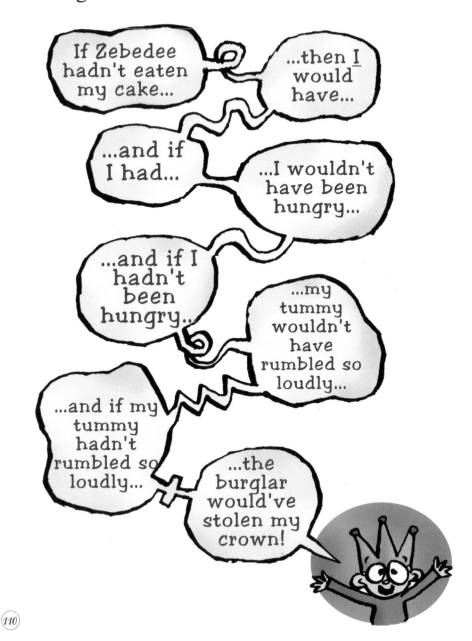

「感謝西庇太！」國王這麼想。

假如西庇太沒有把我的蛋糕吃光……

……那麼我就吃得到蛋糕……

……而如果我吃了……

……就不會肚子餓……

……如果我不餓……

……肚子就不會叫得那麼大聲……

……肚子如果沒叫得那麼大聲……

……那麼，小偷就會偷走我的皇冠了！

The king jumped out of bed and raced over to Zebedee's house in his **pyjamas**.

He found the **Ex**-taster to the king sitting in a corner, looking very sorry for himself.

He was indeed a **sorrowful sight**!

國王立刻跳下床，穿著睡衣跑到西庇太家裏。

他發現這位國王的前任試吃官正坐在牆角，看起來非常懊惱。

真是慘不忍睹！

pyjamas [pə`dʒæməz] 名 睡衣褲

ex [ɛks] 形 以前的

sorrowful [`sɑrofəl] 形 令人悲傷的

sight [saɪt] 名 情景

To Zebedee's surprise the king **strode** over and gave him a big **hug**...

...and a **hearty slap** on the back.

'Thank goodness for Zebedee Zing, the World's Greatest Taster!' said the king, and he told Zebedee all about the burglar.

出乎西庇太的意料之外，國王大步走向西庇太，並給西庇太一個大大的擁抱……

喔！西庇太！

……然後親切地拍著他的背。

「感謝西庇太，你真是全世界最好的試吃官！」國王這麼說著，然後把所有關於小偷的事告訴西庇太。

stride [straɪd] 動 大步走

（過去式 strode [strod]；

過去分詞 stridden [`strɪdn̩]）

hug [hʌg] 名 緊抱

hearty [`hɑrtɪ] 形 誠摯的

slap [slæp] 名 啪地擊打

When he'd finished, the king asked Zebedee to come back to the palace.

'I'd love to!' said Zebedee, because he'd **missed** the king and the palace very much indeed.

'That's true!' said the king.

說完以後，國王要求西庇太回到皇宮。

「我很願意！」西庇太說，因為他真的很想念國王和皇宮。

可是我想你已經不再需要試吃官了！

「沒錯！」國王說。

但是，我有一個更重要的新工作要讓你做！

真的？

miss [mɪs] 動 想念

Chapter Thirteen

$\mathcal{H}$ere's Zebedee in his new uniform...

And here's the king in his new crown (**actually** it's the same crown—he just wrote on it, that's all!)

第十三章

這是西庇太穿著新制服的樣子……

帽子上的'F'是「朋友」的意思……

……而上面的皇冠代表我是國王的朋友!

這是國王戴著新皇冠的樣子（其實是同一頂皇冠，只是國王在上面寫了字而已!）

皇冠上的'F'表示「朋友」……

……而'ZZ'代表我是西庇太的朋友!

actually [ˈæktʃʊəlɪ] 副 實際上

Together they played...

...and watched movies...

...and **splashed** around in chocolate milk!

他們倆人一起玩……

……一起看電影……

……在游泳池裡互相潑著巧克力牛奶！

splash [splæʃ] 動 潑水

And when it came to dinner time, Zebedee ate a little less, and the king ate a little more, more or less...

And the burglar? He was found the very next day, and made to wash up all the big, **greasy** pans in the twelve cooks' kitchen, until he was really, truly sorry...

And so Zebedee Zing and the king lived happily ever after...

吃晚餐時，西庇太就吃少一點，國王則吃多一點，有多有少……

　　至於小偷嘛？第二天就被抓到了，而且被指派到十二位廚師所掌管的廚房裡，負責清洗所有油膩的大鍋子，直到他真心反悔為止……

　　從此以後，西庇太和國王過著幸福快樂的日子……

greasy [`grɪsɪ] 形 沾著油的

...except, perhaps, for when it was time for **dessert!**

……或許，只有一個時候例外——點心時間！

dessert [dɪ`zɝt] 名 甜點

為孩子寫

~ 看的繪本＋聽的繪本　童話小天地最能捉住孩子的心 ~

噓～趕快鑽進被窩，
爸爸媽媽甜蜜的說故事時間就要開始

彩色的夢

🌀 **兒童文學叢書**

童話小天地

國家圖書館出版品預行編目資料

國王的試吃官／Damon Burnard 著／繪；刊欣媒體營
　　造工作室譯－－初版. －－臺北市：三民，民89
　　　面；　　公分
　中英對照
　ISBN 957-14-3267-9（平裝）

　1.英國語言－讀本

805.18　　　　　　　　　　　　　　89010075

網際網路位址　http://www.sanmin.com.tw

©　國王的試吃官

作者兼繪圖者	Damon Burnard
譯　者	刊欣媒體營造工作室
發行人	劉振強
著作財產權人	三民書局股份有限公司 臺北市復興北路三八六號
發行所	三民書局股份有限公司 地址／臺北市復興北路三八六號 電話／二五○○六六○○ 郵撥／○○○九九九八——五號
印刷所	三民書局股份有限公司
門市部	復北店／臺北市復興北路三八六號 重南店／臺北市重慶南路一段六十一號

初版一刷　中華民國八十九年十月
編　號　S85551
定　價　新臺幣貳佰陸拾元整

行政院新聞局登記證局版臺業字第○二○○號

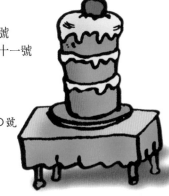

ISBN　957-14-3267-9（平裝）